I0670166

Negro Cowboys: A Long Journey

Looking For My Papa

SARAH ANN FOY

i

Negro Cowboys: A Long Journey Looking My Papa

All rights reserved. No part of this book may be used or reproduced by any means, graphic, electronic, or mechanical, including photocopying, recording, taping or by any information storage retrieval system without permission of the publisher except in the case of brief quotations embodied in critical articles and reviews.

ISBN: **978-0-9963088-2-3**

Original Publication Date: **2001** A.D.

Library of Congress Control Number: 2016913523

Copyright: © **2016 Sarah Ann Foy**

Publisher: 9Ruby Prince Publishing

Executive Editorial: Sean Caddy Amun LinZy I

Champaign, Illinois - United States Of America

Negro Cowboys:
A Long Journey
Looking For My Papa

Sarah Ann Foy

Negro Cowboys:

A Long Journey
Looking For My Papa

From Mississippi to Texas Prison,

"Hey Toby! Stop barking before you's wake up everybody!"

Well the day has finally come for me to make this long trip from home.

"Here boy, here Toby, let's go out quietly cause I know you got to pee!"

I know that I'm going to miss you boy and sorry I can't take you this time. This trip is for men's only, you see and just for a short time.
I hope my friend Charles Henry will be ready for this trip.

The hardest decision for me was should I wake my family up before I leave? I went to my little brother's room and covered him up and went to my mom's room to give

2

her a light kiss on the forehead. I grabbed some grubs and rode off on my horse to get my friend Charles Henry.

Back home I left my worried and broken hearted momma. You see, It's three of us youngins and I am in the middle my older sister Sarah got married at seventeen years old, about four years ago. My baby brother Anthony is fourteen. I left him behind with my momma, Minnie.

My friend Charles Henry is like family, I've known him for over nine years. We have a lot of things in common. Sometimes for example we think a-like, share the same foods we eat, like to hunt and we are always there for each other.

Some folks say that I act older then my age, for whatever that means. We youngins had to do our papa's chores, while he was locked up in a chain gang in Texas.

PREACHER BOY AND CHARLES HENRY

"Hey let's stop and rest in the shade Preacher boy. I reckon we should get some rest. Charles Henry are you ready to turn around and go home.

I knows this has been the longest days in my life and we's halfway there I guess.

You see, me and my friend Charles Henry started out riding for two days ago from Mississippi. We's didn't have no idea how long it's gonna take us or how safe it's going to be!

One day you see, my papa was taking away to prison chain gang camp of something. I was a youngin about eight years old then. One day, these men came to our house. They banged on the door and yelled out so dang loud!

5

I member, I saw my papa sweat like its pouring rain! Now, since I'm about 18 years old, I hafta know if he is alive or what condition he was in.

"Hold it, stop Charles Henry, Whoa boy! Did you see that big ugly thing? What kind of snake was that? Do not move Preacher Boy!

"Oh by the way dats what everybody calls me because I'm always preaching about how I'm going to dat, get rich and find Papa.

"This baby is mines, said Charles Henry and not taking his eyes off the long stripy green and black creature. Boom... Boom! I think I got that sucka Preacher Boy. Hell, I got that sucka.

You know all of the snake killings and hunting, we did together. This was about time to pee my pants! Hey Preacher

Boy, do you think I we can eat him for tonight? After all, I'm tired and hungry and we may not have much of a choice.

"Hey Preacher Boy let's find us a spot so we's can rest for a while. Don't want to wear out our horse's shoes too soon. Neva know if we's hafta find a blacksmith. Look yonder Preacher Boy, over there by the big rock by dat tree there!"

"Hey Charles Henry, it's a good thang. I fetched plenty of matches from home and grabbed some money that my Papa had put away. I guess he was waiting for my time and age to go looking for him.

"Hey! hey! look a jack rabbit between those rocks! Ya gotta think of ours Supper for tonight. We's gotta act real fast to catch dat sucka.

"Com'on Charles Henry, over yonder I saw something in those bushes. What ya'll trying to say boy, that the Jack rabbit is trying to get caught by us. Hell no! maybe he is just as tired as us fools!"

Shhh! Slowly Charles Henry aim that shotgun and shoot with one eye open, man! Boom! I think you got a catch for today, boy!

We later settled down for dat night. We heard all kinds of sounds and I admit me being a man was about to disappear that night. I asked Charles Henry a question trying not to let him learn any hints about me being scared.

"Charles Henry do you miss your mom and dad, boy?"

Charles Henry answered painfully, "Everyday! Preacher Boy and when my grandma is sometimes feeling sickly. But you know what I miss the most about her is her large cuddling arms and saying to me, *'you will make a fine strong man one day.'*

Preacher Boy begins to capture the moment and says, "Oh yeah, she would say, *'see you now with 'please God, let me be that man now!'*

"Funny Preacher Boy, I's know you's shaking in your boots now! Ha, ha!

The boys flame is getting low and also the matches from the other nights before that they used.

Charles Henry responds with tired sleepy eyes,

"I'm gonna turn in now, Preacher Boy cause something tells me, it's gonna get cold."

Preacher Boys nods in agreement, "Yea, me too, after I go and pee somewhere near the bushes."

Charles Henry is fallen heavily into sleep answers,

"Hey, Preacher Boy! You's darker than me, so don't worry about someone seeing you, buddy!"

Preacher Boys laughter fills the air and says, "Ha, ha, I reckon you would have a problem, if you were to pee, cause you would light up in the dark! Ha, ha, back to you.

Before you know it the two nervous young Negro Cowboys fell sound to sleep. By the time the flame did burn out and they snored, scratched and curled up like babies.

Charles Henry looks at his friend and says, "Preacher Boy, how much water do you have left?"

Preacher responds, "I have some that might last me all day. Man as hot as it is, I don't know how much mines is going to last."

Charles Henry adds, "Preacher Boy, Its mighty hot today and it might bake me to the bone."

"You know what Charles Henry", Preacher Boy being sarcastic continues, "if it does, I won't worry about looking for any food. I will just eat you and pick my teeth, ha, ha!"

Charles Henry begins to focus from a distance and says, "Hey Preacher Boy, I see two horses coming, just act like we don't see 'em. Tell me hows you planning to do that?"

Preacher Boy starts to question and says, "how we know if the Injuns is going to kidnap us?"

Charles Henry continues, "Boy hush, there ain't dat many people around attacking peoples. My old rusty knife is all shined up and ready for action.

Preacher Boy implies, "just act normal with a small grin and keep going."

They interact with the riders and Preacher Boy decides to speak up and says, "Howdy Sir, nice day out today!"

As the strangers kept riding past them ignoring the two young cowboys. Preacher Boy was thinking to himself and says, "did we act like we wanted to speak to ya'll anyways?"

He then looks at his friend and says, "Dang Charles Henry some people are not so friendly around the neck of woods."

12

Charles Henry gets excited and says, "Guess what! I see a lake over there. Let's take a cool dive and water our horses."

Me and Charles Henry have been riding for three days now! Some small towns we stopped in and along the countryside. We met some friendly folks who offered some of their grub.

I could see the looks on some folks faces that they were worried about us being by ourselves on this long journey. I have to admit I felt some fear in my bones a time or two.

"Charles Henry! Charles Henry!" Preacher Boy screaming to get his attention continues, "How about stopping and we's figured out our next plan for today. And maybe find out if we's are close to my Papa is!"

Charles Henry is not concentrating on the location and says, "Preacher Boy it is, we are going in circles instead of gidding close! Hey Preacher Boy what if we's is lost and can't find your Papa? I have to admit I'm a little scared and maybe we are not old enough to try looking for Papa, Boy! I am hungry, Preacher Boy! Just dang hungry."

"Me too." Preacher Boy interrupts, "So stop your crying, what we must do is stop at the next house and put on our little act. You know which act is that I am talking about, Charles Henry?"

"Yea, yea! Charles Henry recalling a past agreement and says, "How can I fur get. When I's have to be the one all time buster!"

"But you's know Charles Henry," Preacher Boy recalling memories, "I sho misses Momma's hot skillet water bread and molasses."

Charles Henry is started to feel his stomach reactions and says, "But all your'n doing is making the two of us more hungry!"

"Stop! Charles Henry, I see a sign." Preacher Boy is gaining excited and says, "Read, read Boy! Well it says twenty miles Fort Worth, Texas. I guess that's how you say it, Haleluyah!

Preacher Boy remembers and says, "I think that prisum is near where my Papa is dat called Hunsville.

As we started out, I felt knots rolling up in my stomach.

"Ah, ah Charles Henry, do you sees what I see like a house over yonder?"

"I reckon so Preacher Boy and I guess you'll tell me you's hungry and tired, too!"

"Well you going to follow me are not Charles Henry?"

"You know I's feels the same way you do, Boy! You know that reminds me of when my sister wanted something bad enough, she would kill me by saying, *'Troy Adams, oh that's my real name.'* and she would say, *'you know you want that too or you need it as bad as I do, Boy!'*

You think deez folks will be friendly or have I heads shot off! Charles Henry is this what I will be hearing from you is

16

guessing all the time? Don't you know something sometimes?"

"Well Preacher Boy, I see a barn and a shotgun house. Look, Look, there's a dog with ah gurl."

"I guess Charles Henry don't panic but here comes dat dog and please hold still. Long as dat dog don't spook our horses."

"Preacher Boy, I'm not moving another step until I know we's welcome or not!"

"Well , I guess we will find out cause here she comes. We got to be Mens now!"

The girl approaches the two boys in a soft voice with curiosity and says, "and what are you boys looking for?"

Preacher Boy answers, "Uh, uh, we kind of lost and hungry. And we didn't mean to be causin no trouble man! We beez on our way right, Charles Henry!"

The girl responds, "Boys, where are you heading to and you two kind of young to be traveling by yourselves?"

Charles Henry starts blushing and says, "Oh shucks, we been riding fur twelve days just like men and ain't got a scared bone in our body! You know, we rode from Mississippi to almost Fort Wort that sounds like something a man could do!"

Preacher Boy jumps in the conversation and says, "Man, my friend is running off at the mouth, could you tell us wheres we could git something to eat?"

The girl answers them and says, "I don't think sending you to a proper place to eat cause some folks around here wouldn't take kindly to you. I guess I

18

can gather up some grub for the both of you. But, what I have to do is get you to the barn and hide you two there for now!"

Charles Henry asks, "Well, what about your dog, ma'am Ah she don't look too friendly to me and my friend?"

The girl reassures them, "oh don't worry about Dusty, he is just like family and he usually helps Pa with the horses.

By the way, just call me Elizabeth or Liz. Hurry up and follow me around that barn boys. Hurry, Hurry now stay put and I will fetch you some grub."

There was a voice in the distance yelling, "Elizabeth, Elizabeth!"

"Oh no, that's my Pa," as Elizabeth panics, "and I need to act normal when I come out from this barn! Pa here I come and I won't be late to help Ma."

The voice is heading closer to the barn. "Elizabeth what on earth are you doing in the barn?"

"Nothing Pa! Just checking on my horse and the…ah nevermind! Pa I told you I am coming!"

The voice continues with suspicion, "Liz, now you know that your Ma will worry if you don't show up when she need ya. Hurry up my child so she... she, ah what's that moving in the corner? Liz, do you hear your Papa talking to ya!

"Oh, ah Papa, please don't get angry! Please don't hurt my friends!"

The voice finally ascends into the barn with panic in his voice, "What on earth are they doing in my barn?"

Preacher Boys panics and comes out of hiding and asks, "Sir, uh... uh, I can explain Sir, if you can spare shooo… shooting me and my friend!"

The voice replies with caution, "Okay Boys! Stand there and doncha move ya hear!"

Elizabeth jumps in and pleads, "Pa, please put down the pitchfork!"

The voice gives Elizabeth commands, "Elizabeth go and fetch my shotgun! I think theres something more to this you little negro bucks. Go Liz and fetch your Ma so she can be a witness of you boys possible chance you have violated my

21

daughta.

Fear sets in with the boys and Charles Henry gains courage to speak and says, "No way Sir, we are just traveling thru looking for my friends father in prisum."

The voice responding to the boys and says, "You boys, I can tell ya, betta than I can show ya and besides the Sheriff will make the decision in what to do with ya both."

Elizabeth's Ma calls out to her Papa, "Phil, honey, are ya ok?"

The voice has a name Elizabeth's Papa Phil as he speaks, "Patricia Louise, quick help me tie these two young Negro Bucks in here. Until I can make some arrangements with the Sheriff."

Elizabeth pleads, "Pa... Pa! Please they are innocent! They didn't touch me. These boys are traveling and one of them is looking for his Pa! Pa, please listen about what really happened, I promised them some grub and send them on their way."

"Well Elizabeth," Papa Phil explains, "it's out of my hands right now! When morning come, I will gather them up in the wagon child. If my daugtha is telling the truth and ya betta hope I will be convinced if it's the truth. Sheriff Andrew wouldn't be to pleased to hear such an awful lie. By the way, what is both of you's name boys."

"Ah, ah my name is Charles Henry and this is my friend Preacher Boy."

Papa Phil asks out of interests, "What kind of name is dat for a negro buck? I guess your Papa is a Preacher, huh?"

Preacher Boys speaks out of concern, "Sir, please don't get mad at your daugtha! They call me Preacher Boy and I need to find my Papa dat been in a prisum chain gang since I's about eight years old."

"Boy, no need to talk any mo until tomorro morning."

Charles Henry becomes very nervous and says, "Boy, what a mess you got us in now, Preacher Boy!"

"Hey shut up Charles Henry, it's you he saw standing next to the haystack."

Next day at 9 o'clock am

Papa Phil walks to the barn to speak to the boys, "Get up boys and stand on your feet! We going downtown to see Sheriff Andrew."

By now the boys are scared to death of what happen to them. Preacher Boy had many things going through his head. For one, he is thinking was this trip worth making.

"Ah, ah, Sir! Preacher Boy is pleading with Papa Phil, "please don't have the Sheriff lock us up cause weez done nutin wrong!"

"Hush boy, save your breath until you see Sheriff Andrew. Elizabeth, honey go back to the house girl and stay with your

Ma. Tell her that I'm rounding up horses to take the boys to see the Sheriff. And boys you betta hope he will believe your story!"

Preacher Boy is thinking to himself... boy dat day I will neva fo'gat Speaking of sweating brings back memories of dat time when the Bounty Hunters came for my father...

About 10 o'clock am

The journey we made to town was the longest trip from home like.

"Whoa boy! Papa Phil trying to calm down the horses, "fetch the straps boys and tie the horses to the post. Remember, no wrong moves or disrespecting the Sheriff ya hear boys!"

"Yes, Sir", both boys speak in agreement.

"Boys don't talk until you are told too!"

They begin walking in the building and enters the Sheriffs' office

"Good day Sheriff and not so good,

eitha! I caught these two boys in the barn with my daughta. They tried to convince her…to lie to me!"

The Sheriff begins to observe the two boys to sort out the situation and says, "Well boys, what do you have say about this! But before you try to convince me, what's your names boys? You first boy, let's have it! I don't have all day!"

"My name is Preacher Boy and my friend name is…"

"Hey boy, I only asked your name. What kind of name your mama and papa gives you?"

Preacher Boy clears his throat and says, "Well Sir, my name is just Troy, Jr."

"So it's just Troy, Jr. huh? Now you are next boy, what's yours?"

"Uh, my real name is Charles Henry

the third, Sir!"

"Well at least some one remembers their complete name. Well Phil, what's the story with the Negro cowboys and crime have they committed? And soon my assistant deputy jailer comes back this afternoon, they can spill their guts to him."

Papa Phil responds, "Well, I called my daughta and these negro cowboys hiding out in the barn, after they violated my Elizabeth."

The Sheriff begins to analyze the situation "Is this true boys?

"No Sir" Preacher Boy reacts in fear, "Sheriff, please believe us. We did no such thing!"

The Sheriff then asks, "By the way boys where are you going and coming from in this neck of the woods? Speak up for I have ya hides and lock both of you up and throw away the keys."

"Sir, please" Charles Henry is speaking out in honesty, "we rode all the way from Mississippi to Texas to find Preacher Boy's Papa. Oh, I mean my friend Troy's papa. He's locked up in a prisum chain gang, since he was little."

"Did you boys hurt is daughta and you betta tell the truth?"

Preacher Boy defends himself and says, "Sir, we got scared when Elizabeth's papa called out for her. She went to fetch us some grubs and she told us to hid in da barn."

The Sheriff then asks Papa Phil, "Is that what you saw Phil?"

Papa Phil answers, "All I knows is I called Elizabeth over and over before she was at the barn door. I got suspicious and dats why I went to the barn and head noises stirring around. They tried to make Elizabeth defend for them."

The Sheriff looks over in the boys direction and asks, "Well boys, where is this prisum dat your Papa supposed to be in?"

"Preacher Boys answers, "Ah, Sir, it's in Hunsville, Texas."

"I thought, I would ask again in case you changed your story! Well soon as my assistant Deputy shows up again… for now…"

"Ah, Sir", Preacher Boy implies, "We kinda hungry from a long trip and can you tell me the name of this town?"

The Sheriff speaks in a tone voice, "Hey boys, I will do the asking around here and besides in thirty minutes, Mrs. Valery comes to make her rounds for lunch. Hey, Phil do you have any errands to make in town. I need you to stay over until my assistant Deputy show up.

Papa Phil hesitates and says, "Well Sheriff I do but, I will back in about 1 noon."

The time is now 12:10 noon, Paris, Texas. Deputy shows up.

"Good afternoon Sheriff" The Deputy walks the conversation, "How's things been around here!"

"Well Deputy Troy", the Sheriff greets his Assistant Deputy, "how was your trip coming back? After all, what's the story on the prisoners that I hear from some of the folks? And I feel this is gonna a good one! Deputy Troy, let's go and let you meet these two Negro cowboys and maybe you can talk some sense in them or hear their story."

The Deputy becomes curious, "Oh, okay boss, I'm sure you wouldn't give me nutin, I can't handle."

The Sheriff and Deputy walks into the

room to check out the boys.

"Get up boys", the Sheriff Andrew alarms the boys, "I have someone here I want you to meet. Deputy Troy, I don't know if you remember my friend that has a farm east of here in Meadow Bar Creek. His name is Phil Ervin."

"Oh, yea Deputy Troy remembers, "he is the one that lost some cattles two years ago from rustlers?"

"You got it Troy! Well from Phil's side of the story these boys have possibly violated his daughta, Elizabeth. He found these two in the barn with his daughta. Held them over night before bringing them to town. Troy this doesn't sound too good for these Negro cowboys in these parts. Oh man, Phil Ervin will be back around one noon. We can't let this leak outside this jail. Deputy Troy, I got to make a run and don't forget to let your family know you are back in town."

Deputy Troy begins to engage the two boys in a very stern voice, "What have you two got yourselves in and it doesn't sound to for you, too, Negro cowboys. What in the hell you two coming through these parts alone like this? You know boys, I am tired from my trip and I don't feel like preaching to you!

Preacher Boy responds in shock, "Sir, I don't mean no disrespect but dats what they say about me back home! Dats I always preaching about something and they call me Preacher Boy back home Sir! My real name is Troy Adam Jones and I lives in…"

"Boy! Don't play with me, is that a made up name and I am serious!"

"No Sir, yes Sir! And I lives in Mississippi, too!"

"Boy say no more and do you have a Papa and Momma?"

"Yes Sir, well my momma name is…"

Preacher Boy is realizing the expression on the face of Deputy and starts thinking to himself… "I neva seen anybody with a surprise look with sweat rolling off his head like that before…"

Preacher Boy continues, "Ah, her name is Minnie… and my Papa is locked up in a chain gang."

Deputy Troy interrupts, "Hey that's enough and no more for now, so don't tell anyone about your Papa! I will talk to you later!"

Meanwhile 1:30 pm Papa Phil arrives back t the jail... Deputy Troy pulled Preacher Boy in another room...

"Son, I need to talk to you about something important. I'll try to explain this the besta way I can hope you understand this confusing story I have for you. Son, you are Troy Adams Jones, Jr. I know your mother, your little brother and big sister, Sarah. I know where you live and was born.

I know right now you will hafta be a man at this moment and understand this. Your father did go to a prisum chain gang in Texas when you was about seven or eight. Well son, I am your dad. I only served five years with good behavior.

Son, I have a different life now and

38

started a new family. I wanted so bad to contact your mom and you kids. I was a trade off with a deal from prisum. I can't explain right now and I was assigned to this job in this town in order to get freedom.

Son, there are other things I can't say for now. You know, we have a lot to talk about. I will send a letter back with you to give to your Ma. Let's go and get your friend, Charles Henry and talk to the Sheriff.

Son, one thing! I don't want you to hate me for not coming back into yalls life. Just look you all grown up and now, I guess you a man now? Ha, ha! Charles Henry and you can stand a bath. Maybe a good meal as well!"

Preacher Boy is begging for more answers now and asks, "Pa, I hafta ask you this. Did you forget us anytime or didn't want to see us?

Deputy Troy tries to reconcile, "Son never... never that was in my head, heart or wanted to forget! Now Preach on that, Preacher Man and hurry son."

"Pa, maybe I can move here and help you out, what about that?"

"So after you boys are fed, this will be something we need to talk about. I feel I owe the family that much. One-day boy, you will grow up and see the other side of life."

"Lord knows, it's not an easy thing to explain. My lady always knew about you and what happen to me. I'm not going to turn my back on now. Figuring you need me mo than ever. You got to learn how to provide for you and your momma."

The Conclusion of this story

The Sheriff kept this event quiet from the town. Both Sheriff Andrew and Deputy Troy held their own private small trial inside the jail house. They were both convinced these boys were innocent. Their story seemed to be the true one.

Preacher Boy and Charles Henry left seven days after that. You know, those boys and little Alex made several trips back. After that first long journey. Oh yea, Preacher Boy got help to do repairs at home and also a job at last.

Now dats a real cowboy, fo ya! Charles Henry was glad he made that trip because he felt that he gained a dad as well. For these two cowboys, they grew up real fast! This trip was worth every minute of their lives and hard feelings went away!

To be continued...

Author Sarah Ann Foy
Champaign, Illinois

Negro Cowboys:
A Long Journey To Find My Papa

Preacher Boy: Domeiko Deen
Charles Henry: Tion Posey

email: 9rubyprincepublishing@gmail.com
website: www.9rubyprincepublishing.org

www.ingramcontent.com/pod-product-compliance
Lightning Source LLC
Chambersburg PA
CBHW051558120626
46551CB00013B/1578